SCOTT COLBY

AF268966

Scott Colby

Death in Etobicoke and Other Humorous Tales

First published by Scott Colby 2023

Copyright © 2023 by Scott Colby

All rights reserved. No part of this publication may be reproduced, stored or transmitted in any form or by any means, electronic, mechanical, photocopying, recording, scanning, or otherwise without written permission from the publisher. It is illegal to copy this book, post it to a website, or distribute it by any other means without permission.

Scott Colby asserts the moral right to be identified as the author of this work.

First edition

ISBN: 978-1-9991670-3-5

Cover art by Luke Murphy
Illustration by Maya Remshwar Langston

This book was professionally typeset on Reedsy
Find out more at reedsy.com

*This book is dedicated to those
tasty and tantalizing people and desires in life
that bring us the promise of great pleasure,
but ultimately prove destructive.*

Contents

Preface

Death in Etobicoke and Other Humorous Tales
was originally published
as *Tales from the North Shore* in 2019.

Part III of the Death in Etobicoke trilogy,
"Rebirth in Etobicoke: A Love Story,"
was revised for *Death in Etobicoke and Other Humorous Tales.*

Acknowledgments

This collection of short stories would not have happened if not for the friendship and encouragement of Brett Popplewell, publisher of *The Feathertale Review*. All stories were published in *The Feathertale Review.* Some edits have been made for this publication. Deep thanks to Brett for publishing my fiction and encouraging me to write.

I need to thank and apologize to legendary horror writers Stephen King (*The Shining*), Thomas Harris (*The Silence of the Lambs*), Ira Levin (*Rosemary's Baby*) and even Thomas Mann (*Death in Venice*). The "Death in Etobicoke" trilogy started as a satirical take on *Death in Venice* but then became a tribute to the great works of King, Harris and Levin.

The Thunder Bay trilogy was inspired by the unique characters I met growing up in the Lakehead. "Royal Flush" is fiction but inspired by a real person who worked on Thunder Bay's waterfront and carried a laminated pubic hair in his wallet that he insisted belonged Her Royal Highness. "The Legend of Stump Foot" and "Under the I" are memoirs and are written as truthfully as my memory could recall.

The names in "Under the I" have been changed to protect the innocent but I need to make a special mention of Leo Leclair, the real name of the Volunteer Pool bingo manger. I Googled Leo's name and found a 2007 obituary. Leo lived to be 86. He dedicated his life to the Volunteer

Pool and his two great passions were sports and children. He served six years fighting in the Second World War, I think from age 18 to 24. I wish I had known that when I worked for him, 35 years after the war ended. I would have loved to have talked to Leo about his experiences, assuming he would want to talk about them. So many veterans from that generation did not. Thank you for your service to your community and your country, Leo.

This collection would also not be a reality if not for Jennifer Bazar, who was curator of the Lakeshore Grounds Interpretive Centre in 2019. She made my year when she asked me to read "More Death in Etobicoke: The Silence of the Pigeons" as part of the centre's exhibit "In the Wake of the Passenger Pigeon." Her invitation inspired me to finish the "Death in Etobicoke" trilogy and publish this collection.

I could not have published the book, as well, without the encouragement and talent of artist and designer Luke Murphy, who designed the book cover. I think it was his idea to finish the "Death in Etobicoke" trilogy and self-publish it. Thank you Luke for your skills, inspiration and friendship.

Finally, thanks to my wife Natasha for her continued support and love and to my kids Popcorn and Sweet Pea for their love and inspiration. I hope they enjoy these stories someday.

Special thanks to Maya Rameshwar Langston for her inspired illustration of Lucy Fehr. I hope this is the first of many book covers for Maya.

I

Death in Etobicoke Trilogy

1

Death in Etobicoke: Or How Thomas Mann Inspired the Ultimate Sacrifice for my Book Club

Originally published in The Feathertale Review, Vol. 4

Subject: Book Club Reminder

From: Dr. Jill Jones

Hello devoted book clubbers, just a friendly reminder of the book club next Friday at my place. The book is *Death in Venice* by Thomas Mann. It was Richard's choice. Personally, I'm loving it: A dense, intense read for these cold, dark, intense times.

Jill

* * *

Subject: Re: Book Club Reminder

From: Scott Colby

Thanks, Jill. I'm really enjoying the book too. Earlier this week, after an arduous night cataloging the world's grief and tragedy for *Toronto Star* readers to digest over croissants and coffee the next morning, I lit a candle for ambiance and crawled into bed around 1:30 a.m. with my cat Sushi and the carefully crafted prose of Herr Mann.

His descriptive writing and a still somewhat cryptic plot quickly lured me into another realm, one of sublime near-consciousness. As my eyelids fluttered before the pages, cast in a warm glow of the candle, I battled against the urge to pull the covers up to my chin, blow out the light and listen to the soothing sounds of Lake Ontario waves crashing against the December-chilled rocks outside my open window. The reality between lake-side Etobicoke apartment and gondola-guided canals of Venice were blurring into one mysterious watery world — until the delicate pages of this classic slipped from my relaxing fingers. With an undignified slap, it struck the parquet floor beside my mismatched Sleep Country Canada mattress and box spring, frightening my supine and elongated furry bedmate.

Relying on instincts bred into his feline brain over several millennia, Sushi sprang into motion, like a loaded spring, his powerful hind legs and claws digging into the blue- quilted bedspread, then the soft, pinky flesh of my chest and abdomen, before thrusting himself in an elegant arc over the bed and onto the dresser. He skidded as he landed on the polished oak top of the antique dresser, his left hip gently brushing the candle before gracefully regaining his balance and gliding off into the darkness, landing on the floor and scampering into the safety of the hallway.

As I clutched at my chest, I tried to ignore the searing pain, but the small crimson spot growing on my T-shirt wouldn't let me. Like a cigarette being held to my sternum, the gash burned and the spot continued to spread. My preoccupation with my own pain distracted me from the wobbling candle that had now slipped off the dresser into my clothes hamper. It took a while for me to appreciate the crackling, warm glow emanating from behind the dresser, like a beach bonfire on a cool summer evening. I had little time to enjoy the ambiance before the magic moment was disrupted by the sharp screech of the fire alarm.

The smoke was getting thicker, making it difficult to breathe. I was confused dealing with the pain, the blood, the screeching alarm, the throat-choking smoke and the flames, now licking at the clothes in my closet. I could hear commotion in the hallway as my neighbours, few of whom I've met yet, scrambled from their slumbers and pulled on coats. Soon, there was a knock on my door.

The smoke had seeped through the cracks. In my grey Stanfields and thread-bared, blood-soaked Detroit Tigers T-shirt, I flipped the latch and greeted my concerned neighbours. Sushi darted through the door and down the stairwell.

The neighbours choked back the billowing smoke and urged me to get out. A matronly Scottish woman in her housecoat grabbed me by the elbow and said, "Come on, laddy, we've got to get you out of here." I took a step for the door, but paused. Looking back into the pulsating orange and black apartment, I said, "No, I need to get my book. Book club is just over a week away" and I darted back into the inferno.

Scott

* * *

Subject: Re: Book Club Reminder

From: Dr. Naomi Boxer

Scott, you are an intensely committed book-clubber! Next time I feel fatigue after a long week in the clinic, I will think of your heroism and will drag myself to the meeting. Unfortunately, I'll be out of town next weekend.

* * *

Subject: Re: Book Club Reminder

From: Scott Colby

Sorry you can't make the next meeting, Naomi.

I'm currently at Trillium Health Centre in a full body cast and in traction, but the ladies auxiliary has agreed to take shifts reading the charred, tattered book to me. I forget where I'm at in the book. I believe he has checked into a hotel after arguing with a gondolier. Oh yeah, he was admiring the perfection of a young Polish boy. I can't wait to find out what happens next!

* * *

Subject: Re: Book Club Reminder
From: Dr. Jill Jones
We are so glad you're alive! We have no doubt in the healing power of a good book. All the best with the body cast.
Jill

* * *

Subject: Re: Book Club Reminder
From: Scott Colby
Thank you Jill for the kind words and encouragement.
In what is being considered some sort of medical miracle, my cast is expected to be removed soon. The ladies auxiliary is enjoying the book tremendously, as well. Between reading chapters to me they enjoy massaging my feet, the only exposed part of my body at the moment. This literary classic is a particular hit with the young lady who dresses like a Goth, in all black with heavy black eyeliner and a pierced nose, lip, tongue, eyebrows and I dare not ask where else. There is something about an exhausted, depressed, knighted German aristocrat's obsession with a

blonde god-like Polish boy with perfect skin but "weak teeth" that has her staying long after visiting hours have ended. Whatever germicide the Venetian officials are pouring into the canal I'm sure the custodial staff at the hospital is using to disinfect the equipment. See you all in a week.

* * *

Subject: Re: Book Club Reminder
     From: Dr. Delilah Doherty
     Jill, as always, you help us find the bright side of life!
     Just think, Scott, without reading this book, you would never have experienced the love of your neighbours, the dedication of Trillium's health-care providers, the tender care of volunteers. You would never know what it's like to be a truly captive audience ... or the freedom of release from captivity (It's coming!)
     Delilah

* * *

Subject: Re: Book Club Reminder
     From: Scott Colby
     Dear Jill, Naomi, Delilah, Richard and the rest of the gang.

You are all correct. The book seems to have taken on a mystical quality inside the antiseptic confines of the Trillium Health Centre.

The cleaning staff in their long, white gowns, crisp white paper hats, paper masks tied tightly behind tucked-in hair and their Sleep Country Canada white paper booties have been scurrying around here like a colony of ivory ants. The odour of the Venetian-like germicide is ever present. It's not heavy and suffocating as the sirocco plaguing Venice, but constant, nonetheless, like the inevitability of the changing seasons, or the rising and setting of the sun. I'm sure they are using the same agent to scour every now-spotless corner, every seam in every tile, the top of every piece of institutional furniture, every nook and cranny of every stainless steel instrument they use to poke and probe at my remarkably healing skin and bones. But the blackened and battered copy of Thomas Mann's *Death in Venice and Other Tales* remains untouched by the diligent cleaning staff.

Even the doctors and nurses don't touch it. I'm not sure if it's out of reverence for the masterpiece, how it and I miraculously survived the fire, or in its daily and highly anticipated role in my healing. However, sometimes I detect caution towards it, as one ignores a wasp, aware of its potential for pain, but fairly sure it will fly harmlessly away.

The book sits untouched beside my bed until the afternoon arrival of my Gothic ladies auxiliary volunteer. The others have stopped coming. I haven't been told why. It is only her now. But I don't mind. In fact, her presence is the only event I look forward to, more so than the removal of the cast and the bandages and the application of the healing ointments. I have come to crave her arrival. I need it as much as I need food, oxygen or water. She arrives at the same time in the late afternoon as the sun hangs low in the December sky, but it is always a surprise when she arrives at the door, a stealthy figure in black set against the stark, white hospital walls. A smile never cracks her thin, painted black lips, but there is a hypnotic welcoming in her clear, sharp, grey eyes, dramatically framed by her thick black eyeliner and black, studded piercings. I know very little about her. My journalistic questioning is politely deflected. She has at least offered me her name. It is Lucy. Lucy Fehr.

Lucy always takes off her long, black trench coat and hangs it perfectly on the hanger, revealing her knee-high black Doc Marten boots, tight black jeans with the random holes and rows of safety pins, her tight-fitting black T-shirt and soft jet-black hair that cascades over her shoulders. Her uniform of black clothing and various piercings contrasts with what little I can see of her flawless, young alabaster skin. At this time of day, the soft afternoon winter sun gives her skin the affect of self-illumination, like that of an angel.

To me, Lucy has become an angel, a much anticipated distraction from the daily monotony of lying in a hospital bed. There seems to be fewer and fewer people in the hospital, except for the ubiquitous cleaning staff. The few doctors, nurses and the rare visitor all seem to be wearing paper masks. They gather in the hallways in small clusters, murmuring with apparent concern, but I can't decipher their muffled offerings. The casts were removed yesterday, the wounds cleaned and I've been given fresh dressings. The doctors feel I can go home soon, yet, despite my miraculous physical improvements, I have been feeling weak, lethargic and unsettled the past few days.

That is until the arrival of my black and white angel, a perfect study in contrasts, like piano keys; yin and yang personified. Her slender white fingers, tipped with elongated, immaculate, black fingernails, confidently holds the singed, fragile book. We finished *Death in Venice* a few days ago but she continues to return, as sure as the sun sets every evening, delving into Mann's other stories, such as "The Blood of the Walsungs" about siblings who have sex under the influence of Wagnerian opera, or "Gladius Dei" where the main character is horrified by fleshy, erotic paintings he considers blasphemous. Lucy's rhythmic voice often lulls me into a blissful state, where I seem to float just above my mattress; an auditory Lorazepam, if you will, that leaves me straddling reality. As she continues in her soft, hypnotic voice she sometimes appears to be translating the text back into its original German. Yet, I understand every word.

The doctor has returned. Behind her stark white gown and mask, she is confident I can leave today, this afternoon if I want. She almost insists. Lucy suddenly appears, a black figure centred within the white door frame. "Tomorrow. I'll leave tomorrow."

I'm relieved to see her, but I'm still a little weak and faint. There is concern in the doctor's eyes and she says she will check on me later. Perhaps this evening I will feel well enough to leave.

"Yes, I'm sure you'll be leaving soon," Lucy softly states, as she picks up the black Penguin Classic with the darkened pages and settles beside me.

The doctor leaves, promising to return in a few hours. As Lucy reads, her pure, white skin, softly lit by the setting sun, slowly disappears into the shadows of her raven

hair as the winter sun sinks into the watery crypt of Lake Ontario. The room darkens. The hospital is oddly quiet. Lucy is now just a silhouette against a window that is painted by a twilight sky. Lucy's luring voice rhythmically sounds out words "... der führer des geistes lächelte an ihm von heraus dort und winkte zu ihm ..."

The room is draped in blackness, the darkest dark before the dawn. Blackness is followed by more blackness. A complete blackness that blankets all things. Time stops. There is no present, no past and no future. Just blackness. Eternal, all-encompassing blackness.

Then, a small pinpoint of light appears. An intense, penetrating point of light. It slowly grows into a widening beam of the whitest, most blinding light imaginable. It spreads in all directions and envelops all aspects of awareness. Bright, spectacular whiteness everywhere. It lifts me up, embraces me, and bathes me in its brilliance.

2

More Death in Etobicoke: The Silence of the Pigeons

(Originally published in The Feathertale Review, Vol. 20)

"Come on Siri, one more time!" The anger and desperation in my voice was unmistakable, even to my phone. "Where the hell is Mimico Self-Storage?"

"OK, calm down," Siri shot back in that annoying robotic voice, dripping with fake cheer and sincerity. "I found fifteen places called Mimico Self-Storage."

"Are you kidding me? I. Just. Need. One," I growled.

My iPhone glowed in the darkness of my minivan, but I couldn't read the small type without my reading glasses, which were packed away, somewhere.

Whoa! I gripped the wheel harder as the van skidded again on the snowy backstreets.

I looked at my iPhone again and squinted as I typed in the passcode: 733786. Then I tapped the green message button and scrolled, trying to find that text from Richard. I found it and squinted at it, struggling to read his text.

"Mimico Self Storage. 333 Overlook Ave. Off Judson, near the jail."

"Richard," I muttered to myself. "You fool, there is no Overlook Ave. in South Etobicoke."

"I'm sorry, I didn't get that?"

"Shut up Siri! You're no help to me!"

"That's not very nice."

I threw my phone onto the passenger seat and peered out into the flying snow. Sleet pounded the windshield, slowly winning the battle against my wipers. I was lost in the night, wandering through a blizzard in some God-forsaken Toronto industrial park — near a prison.

Ice slowly overtook the windshield, making it nearly impossible to read the street signs. The darkness of yet another winter storm smothered almost any illumination from the street lights. The console mounted on the van ceiling read: 6:27 p.m. Above that: NE -17C.

I was pretty sure the last sign I read said Magnificent Rd. The irony! The city planning department had a good sense of humour. The summer tires skidded on the ice and struggled to plough through the growing drifts as I inched along. Slowly a sign emerged through the storm, but I could barely make it out through the windshield. I lowered the side window a crack. A blast of arctic air hit my face. I could read the word "Mimico" but nothing else. I squinted at it as snow and ice slapped my cheeks and forehead. Then I saw the most curious thing. A pigeon perched on top of the sign.

What was a pigeon doing up there in this weather?

As I crept down the street beyond the sign the words "Self storage" slowly revealed themselves on another sign, followed by an arrow pointing to a lane that disappeared behind an abandoned gas station. There it was: Overlook Avenue — easily overlooked. I put on my turn signal, for who to see I wasn't sure and ventured into the laneway. It twisted to the right behind the gas station, then left behind an imposing iron and glass warehouse, then left again and then right. Large mirrors were tucked into each corner of the darkened lane, meant to reflect oncoming traffic. But there was no one else out here. Just me and the streaks of vertical white sleet illuminated by my headlights, framed in blackness.

A dark, grey building appeared at the end my headlights' reach, along with yet another sign high on a pole, topped by the silhouette of what I swear to God appeared to be yet another pigeon lost in the storm. The small parking lot was empty and I pulled up to the one-storey office, which was attached to quite a large two-storey aluminum- sided warehouse. The building was wide and deep, with a peaked roof for each row of storage lockers. I marvelled at how a building of this size fit back here. A single light illuminated the inside of the office and I could see the shadow of a woman sitting behind a desk.

I grabbed my phone and began to text Richard. "Richard I've arrived. Finally found self-storage you suggested."

I punctuated the message with my usual smiley face emoji and pressed send. But it didn't send. I tried again. Nothing. One more time. Still nothing. And then:

WHAM!

Something smashed against my windshield. I jumped back in my seat. Another wham. There was something out there, clinging to the wiper, fluttering against the windshield. My heart started beating harder as I turned off the wipers. I wanted to see what it was. There was a tap against the window. Then another tap. And another.

The hair on my neck stood up and my chest tightened. I hollered: "Who's out there?"

There came no answer but for the unmistakable sound of ice scraping away from glass.

"Who's out there?" I yelled again into the windshield.

No response, only the sound of more scraping. A hole slowly appeared in the layer of ice frozen onto my windshield. I leaned forward and looked through the hole only to see what appeared to be — a beak? I hunched over the steering wheel and peered ever closer through the small hole in the ice. There was more scraping and then nothing. I leaned up against the window and pressed my face to the hole. I couldn't believe my eyes — or my eye, in this case. A demonic-looking pigeon with a fiery red eye was staring back at me.

I jolted back into my seat and flicked the wipers on full speed, launching the wicked-looking bird off my windshield and back into the howling wind and snow. It disappeared into the blizzard. I shivered in my seat, more from the creepiness than from the cold. This bizarre encounter had unsettled me and I paused to catch my breath. When finally I felt brave enough to slip on my gloves and toque I climbed out of the van, looking around before making for the light inside the office.

The door chime, a flock of metal pigeons, rang as I burst inside the building, blown through by the storm. A woman with long, straight hair lifted her head from a tattered copy of *Death in Venice* by Thomas Mann. It looked as if it had been pulled out of a camp fire. She sat with her body concealed behind the counter from her leather-coated shoulders down. Her hair was as dark as midnight, a stark contrast against her flawless ivory skin. Her deep almond-shaped eyes were as black as coal and were framed by equally black eyeliner. Her nose was slender and pierced. She was hot and also kind of freaky.

A slow hypnotic smile spread across her thin black-painted lips, revealing a glimpse of eerily white teeth.

"Oh good," she said in a low but welcoming voice. "We've been expecting you."

"Ah, really? Did, um, Richard call for directions?" I asked, unzipping my jacket and shaking ice and snow off my toque.

"Richard?" she said slowly, a questioning brow rising as she spoke. "There's no Richard. No phones, either. On account of the weather."

She dropped the brow and looked out at the storm. "The newspaper says this month has been the coldest in recorded history."

"Then how were you expec ... oh never mind. I was hoping to rent a heated storage locker. I need to drop off some boxes from my van. The rest is arriving from Colorado in a few days. I have I.D. if you need it."

She pushed back her chair and stood up, revealing a tight-fitting, black-studded leather jacket with black leather pants, so form-fitting they looked as if they had been sewed around her legs. Her black leather boots came up to her knees. All she was missing was a riding crop. She had an alluring, yet intimidating presence; it was distinct, yet oddly familiar. I tried not to stare.

"No need, Mr. Colby," she said, leaning toward me. "Here are your forms to sign." She slid the papers across the counter.

Mr. Colby? How did she ...?

I looked at the forms. They'd been prepped and personalized before my arrival. This night was getting weirder by the moment. Then I noticed the illustration of a pigeon on the letterhead.

"What's with the pigeons?" I asked.

She gripped the counter in her hands and leaned her body backwards as if she were inhaling my question.

"*Ectopistes migratorius*," she purred.

"Pardon me?"

"The spirit of the past permeates this place, Mr. Colby."

Her head now tilted toward a framed watercolour portrait of a pigeon behind her desk. The pigeon in the portrait was striking, like nothing I'd seen. A blue head and tail, red breast and matching red eyes.

"*Ecto —?*"

"*—pistes migratorius*," she repeated, more softly and smoothly than before. "A passenger pigeon, also know as the wild pigeon. Once estimated to be the most populous bird in North America, if not the world. Two-hundred years ago there were at least three billion of these birds in the sky."

I didn't know what to say so I said the only thing that came to mind. "Huh."

"To put that in perspective, that is about a third the number of birds in North America today. The males were a stunning slate-blue with wine-red undersides

and a touch of purple. The females were not quite as flamboyant. The ornithologist John James Audubon once witnessed a mile-wide flock of migrating pigeons blocking the sun for three full days as they passed overhead."

The more she talked about the birds the more entrancing she became.

"One account written from 1855 in Ohio," she continued, "recalled a 'growing cloud' that eclipsed the sun as it approached the city of Columbus. Screaming children sprinted for home. Horses bucked their riders and fled. Women hiked up their long skirts and scurried in fear into stores. Some people dropped to their knees and prayed."

"Why have I never heard of this?" I asked, forgetting, momentarily, why I was here.

"Greedy and clueless farmers and hunters destroyed the nesting grounds of these magnificent birds and hunted the flocks with unmatched brutality. Birds were shot, beaten with rakes and potatoes, caught in nets, and asphyxiated with sulfur. Entire roosts were torched and corn heaps poisoned with whiskey."

I still didn't know what to say, so I tried to make sense of her remarkable story. "The pigeons must have been a real nuisance, I guess."

She sniffed at my comment and continued. "After witnessing a great massacre in 1880, Pokagon, a leader of the Potawatomi Nation, could only imagine what divine retribution might be awaiting those who sought to eradicate the flock in favour of the horizon. By 1900, no passenger pigeons survived in the wild. The last of their kind succumbed in captivity in the Cincinnati Zoo, found dead on the floor of its cage on Sept. 1, 1914. Her name was Martha. She was 29 years old."

I was stunned by both the insanity of the pigeon history and by her ability to recount it. I stared at the portrait of the pigeon and it stared at me, as did the woman. All I could muster was an inarticulate, "Holy shit."

"*Sanctus stercore*," she said, letting out a soft, yet discernible, coo.

I struggled to understand the senseless tragedy of this story and why it meant so much to a modern Goth and a self-storage business in a South Etobicoke industrial park. So I asked: "Why is your mascot a tragically extinct pigeon?"

"I'm glad you asked," she said, her voice low, almost buttery. "The name 'Mimico' is derived from the Ojibwa word *omiimiikaa*, meaning 'abundant with wild pigeons.' Passenger pigeons used to gather by the hundreds of thousands at the mouth of the Mimico Creek before migrating across Lake Ontario. This portrait behind me is of Martha, the last of her kind," she said, pointing to the dove-like bird sitting on a branch. "Named after Martha Washington."

"And my name is Lucy," she offered, extending her hand. Her long alabaster fingers, tipped with perfectly manicured black nails, reached across the counter.

"Lucy Fehr."

It was an unsettling name. I tried not to flinch.

"You can have the storage unit 217. Your usual code, the one you use on your phone, it will not work here."

"What? How do you—?"

"It has been taken, by Charles."

"Who is Charles?"

"He hasn't been seen around here in years," she said. "Yet, his billing is still paid by credit card every month. He's in unit 237. I have given you another code."

Her voice was so seductive that I quickly forgot how disturbing it was that she knew the code to my iPhone.

"For you, it will be your code backwards."

She handed me a map of the site and pointed to where I needed to drive.

"The office is closing now," she said, abruptly, yet buttery still and mixed with a tone of irony. "Good night, Mr. Colby. I hope we meet again."

The way she said that last bit seemed to suggest that we may never meet again. I was still somewhat shaken by the storm and the disturbing bird outside. I wasn't yet sure what to make of this Gothic minx who seemed to share her namesake with Satan.

I hurried out into the cold. She locked the door behind me and turned out the lights. I fumbled in my jacket pocket for my keys and struggled to put on my toque as the wind and snow battered my face. When I looked back, Lucy was sitting behind her desk, in the darkness, reading her book again.

I battled through the howling wind to my van and climbed inside, then drove with my chin hovering over the steering wheel, eyes peering through the hole scratched clear by the manic pigeon.

I approached the security gate and pulled up beside the key pad. I typed in the reversed code to my iPhone, just as Lucy instructed: 6-8-7-3-3-7. I half expected nothing to happen but suddenly the chain link fence rolled back, disappearing into a growing snow bank. I eased the van gingerly up an icy ramp to a second-level loading dock, shielded, at least partially, from the storm. I could hear the wind battering against the metal walls of the storage facility as I climbed out of my van, grabbed my boxes and pushed through a steel door into a lighted foyer, beyond which I could only see the beginning of a long, dark hallway.

I stood in the foyer's light for a few seconds, unsure of what to do. I contemplated turning back for my van but was halted by a growing hum. My presence seemed to have triggered a sensor and one by one a string of fluorescent lights popped to life, slowly illuminating a section of the long hallway, revealing hundreds of identical blue metal doors cut into a seemingly endless white metal wall.

I began counting out the lockers as I searched for 217. I walked straight, then turned right down a hall and walked past two dark corridors with more rows of blue metal doors before turning left, then right and left again. The light disappeared behind me as I walked, the sensors only illuminating what lay ahead until, finally, I reached my unit.

I pulled the latch and the metal door creaked open. The unit was 5 feet by 10 feet and was clean, dark and empty. I stacked my two boxes of clothes in the corner and walked the dark hallways back to the exit.

I turned a corner and in the dimness of a distant security light saw the outline of a dolly. Perfect, I thought. This would save me a few trips and strain on my back.

I wheeled the dolly out to the van and loaded up more boxes. As I rolled the next load of possessions though the maze, the metal skin of the building groaned and cracked under the weight of the polar storm pounding outside. Could this place be any creepier?

I reached my unit once more, slid back the latch and stacked more boxes against the back wall.

"Uh," I grunted as a lifted a box of books. I spun around to face the locker but the box hit the dolly and I lost my grip. The box fell on the concrete floor and broke open.

"Just great!" I gathered the books, a collection of American literature: *Old Man and the Sea*, *Lolita*, *Catcher in the Rye*. I put them back in the box, which was now broken, but still managed to contain all the books, but one — *The Shining*. I stacked the broken box on of a pile of other boxes and carefully placed my tattered old dog-eared and coffee stained copy of Stephen King's most horrifying tale on top.

One more trip should do it, I thought. I closed the door and slid the latch. I turned down a darkened hall and waited for the sensor to detect my movement.

The lights clicked on and as I rolled the dolly down the hall, I noticed a feather stuck to one of the wheels. I bent down and peeled it off the black rubber. It was a pretty little feather, the colour best described as wine-red. I let it go and watched it float to the floor before walking on. I rounded the corner and suddenly stopped.

I thought I heard something.

Yes.

There was a sound.

Tick, tick, tick ... tick, tick ... tick, tick, tick tick ... tick.

It was a faint, irregular rhythm coming from the next hall.

Tick, tick, tick ... tick, tick... tick, tick, tick ... tick ... tick, tick.

A typewriter? I hadn't heard that sound in years. Decades.

I left the dolly and walked slowly down the hall toward the sound of letters and thoughts hammering onto the page. But for some reason as I walked down this new hall the overhead lights did not come on. My only illumination was a light escaping into the hallway from inside one of the units. I carefully approached the light and the unit. The door — No. 237 — was slightly ajar. I peeked into the unit.

Tick, tick, tick, tick … tick, tick … tick, tick, tick, tick, tick.

A strange looking man sat at a small desk, his large pointed nose, almost like a beak, hovered over what appeared to be a century-old Smith Corona. His dark hair, streaked with silver, was unkempt and ruffled. Wooden crates were stacked against the back wall, hard-covered books scattered about, including what looked like my exact copy of *The Shining*, dog ears, coffee stains and all. There were also a few clothing racks, an antique bird cage, two identical tricycles and a mannequin.

He spotted me in the corner of his beady little eye and rotated his head in my direction. He stopped typing, opened his thin lips and spoke with a sing-song cadence like none I had heard before.

"This IS a NICE suuurprise. I did not EXPECT to see ANYBODY tooonight," he warbled.

He hopped to his feet and with a jerky motion walked toward me. His head bobbed forward and his leg kicked back with each step. Then he opened his arms wide and extended his hand.

"My name IS Chaaarles," he clucked, as his head bobbed back and forth.

His skin was cold and rough.

"Hi, I'm Scott. Can I ask what are you writing?"

"OH, it's nooothing. Just a historical book I've BEEN peeecking away aaat. I've had writers BLOCK and decided to roooost here FOR a whiiile. Away from ANY distraaactions."

He flapped his arms and crowed: "Come IIIN!"

I paused, thinking it was probably best I leave, but something about the mannequin piqued my interest. It seemed to be covered in grey-blue and red boas.

"What's that?" I asked, pointing to the mannequin. "Thaaat? Just A suuuit."

"Are these feathers?"

"You COULD saaay that."

"Is this a *bird suit*?" I asked in disbelief.

"Oh, it IS, it IS," Charles chirped. His head bobbed back and forth as he turned toward me. Suddenly a wine-red feather popped out of his mouth. "And NOT just aaany bird suuuit," Charles trilled. "*Causa columbae offered.*"

"What?"

"YOU'LL seeee," he hooted as his eyes turned a frightening red.

"I'm ALMOST dooone," he squawked, rubbing his boney hands together. "I have A NAME for her."

"Oh yeah?"

"It's Latin FOR miiistress," he cawed as another wine-red feather popped out of his mouth and slowly floated to the floor. "Miiistress of THE sky."

I was slowly backing up now toward the door. Charles took a step forward, staring with his fiery red eyes. His thin lips drew into a sinister smile as his head continued to bob back and forth.

I bumped into something. It was the typewriter table. I glanced at the page to see what he'd been writing. The same line was typed over and over: "Birds of a feather flock together."

"COO ROO–C'TOO–COO!"

Charles screeched as he strutted toward me. Wine–red feathers popping out of his mouth.

I spun around and began to run but was startled by the deafening sound of drumming wings; furious sounding feathers beat against each other. I felt a rush of wind against my cheeks and inhaled the musty smell of birds.

"COO ROO–C'TOO–COO! COO ROO–C'TOO– COO!"

A flurry of blue and red feathers — everywhere and those red eyes.

"Lucy? Is that you?" I screamed.

"No, Mr. Colby. I am Martha — Queen of the Wild Pigeons."

3

Rebirth in Etobicoke: A Love Story

(Originally published in The Feathertale Review, Vol. 23.)

A pink sticky note was affixed to the front door of our house. Kristin loved those pink sticky notes. Why didn't she just text me? As I walked up the stairs and onto the porch, the words came into focus: *Scott, I'm leaving you. I don't love you anymore.*

I peeled the note off the door and examined it. It was Kristin's handwriting, precise and flowing. The beauty of her script belied the cruelty of her words.

No, correction: YOU are leaving ME. I'll have your stuff sent to you. Once you have a place, text Terry the address.

I stood on my porch with the pink note stuck to my index finger and looked around — what I was looking for, I was not sure. Confusion slowly gave way to anger and my face was suddenly hot. My hand was trembling as I tried to slide the house key into the lock. It didn't fit.

I walked over and peered into the front window. The curtains were drawn. There were no lights on. I was not sure what to do next.

Terry. My best friend. What did he have to do with this? I paced back and forth and as I put my hand to my forehead I noticed Kristin's writing on the back of the note.

Terry and I are in love. It's best for all of us if you just get over it, K?

Kristin and Terry? Get over it? Kristin was ending our marriage with a pink sticky note?

Get over it? Sure, okay! I mean, K! There, that was easy, I told myself — through clenched teeth.

* * *

One door closed (or had the locks changed?) and another one opened. This one, sans life-destroying pink sticky notes, opened into a spartan (Kijiji code for unfurnished and dingy) one-bedroom apartment above a seedy bar in west Toronto. New Toronto, actually — a blue-collar village on the shores of Lake Ontario that dates back to the nineteenth century. It was my new home. My landlady Minnie, who owned the bar and the building, told me The Shore, as it was sometimes called, had been slowly gentrifying for the last one hundred and thirty years.

"Do you think they could hurry things up a bit?" I asked her. She didn't seem to find it funny.

It was almost midnight on a summer Sunday. The bar downstairs, named Romans, depressed me, but I couldn't stand the thought of being in my apartment any longer. I opted to go downstairs for one drink — a decision I soon came to regret.

The place was nearly empty. I sidled up to the battered oak bar and sat on a hard stool. There was a baseball game on the TV. A woman with long black hair was crouched behind the bar, her back to me as she put beer bottles in a fridge. Then she rose, revealing a black lace dress that loosely covered a black crop top that flowed down over black spandex shorts, laced at the sides to expose a touch of skin at her hips. Black leather stiletto boots reached her knees, completing the look. She sensed me staring at her and turned. She smiled through painted black lips and a lip piercing that matched the one in her nose. Everything about her was black or white.

"Welcome aboard," she purred. "We've been expecting you."

What the hell? Was I on *The Love Boat?* This mesmerizing bartender did kind of look like a Goth version of Julie the cruise director. She grabbed three ice cubes, slipped them into a tumbler, poured a generous amount of Canadian Club and slid it across the bar.

"What the? How did you know my drink?"

She looked at me with hypnotic eyes and offered a barely perceptible smile. I raised the glass and took a sip. The whiskey hit my mouth and throat, burning and soothing at the same time.

"Nicely played," I said in a low voice with an enigmatic accent, trying to sound suave like James Bond. It fell flatter than a Finnish pancake. I tried to recover. "Where are my manners? My name is Scott." I smiled.

"I know, Mr. Colby," she replied coldly. "I'm aware of your arrival. And my name is not Julie. It's Lucy. Lucy Fehr."

What is happening? Did she just say her name was Lucifer?

"You should visit here more often," Lucy said. Well, more like demanded. She glared straight into my retinas with her dark, mesmerizing eyes. Suddenly, it felt like she was probably right.

"Yes, Lucy, maybe I should." I shook my head to break her stare and scanned the dark, empty bar, but I could not avoid her eyes.

"Everything happens for a reason, Mr. Colby," she said, her eyes never leaving me, like a tractor beam that penetrated my soul. "There is a reason your wife cheated on you. There is a reason you were brought to The Shore. There is a reason we met tonight."

I caught myself nodding uncontrollably. It felt, for a moment, as though she were controlling my bodily functions. I couldn't breathe. I couldn't talk. Lucy reached across the bar and placed my hand in hers. Her skin was soft, her hand strong — and cold.

"There are no coincidences, Mr. Colby." She was terrifying — and I loved it. What the hell was wrong with me? She winked and changed the topic. "How are you enjoying your apartment?"

How was I enjoying my apartment? How does someone enjoy a root canal? Or stubbing your toe on the coffee table? Or having your wife leave you for your best friend? Correction: your *best man*! The apartment was a hellhole and my life was being flushed down its rust-stained toilet. How did I end up this way? I'd had a marriage, a nice house, a career. But it had all been an illusion. I realized I didn't know what was real anymore. Get a grip, Scott. Don't let her smell the defeat and desperation.

"Well, it is a step down from my home where my wife is living with my former best friend," I said. "It's all I can afford at the moment. But things will turn around soon. I'm expecting an advance on my next book."

That was not completely true. I did desperately need that advance, but it had been a few years since any publishers had shown interest in my manuscripts.

"A writer is a sexy career."

"I'm glad you feel that way," I stammered.

"Tell me about your manuscript."

"It's a horror story set at a remote fly-in fishing lodge in Northwestern Ontario. It's called *Hooked*, and it's about a prostitute who —"

"Ah, that's enough," Lucy interrupted, waving a finger. "I want to be surprised. I like surprises. Do you like surprises, Mr. Colby? I hope it has a twist ending. Those are the best endings. Do you like those endings?"

"Yeah, of course. I'm still working on the ending, actually. I have two endings and I can't decide which one to go with. There is the expected happy resolution, but I have been toying with an ending where the bad guy —"

She slapped the bar and cut me off. "Ah, naughty boy! What did I tell you, Mr. Colby? Don't say any more. But I do like the endings where the bad guy gets away with it, if that's what you're thinking."

* * *

A week later, I was lying on the couch in my apartment, staring at the water stains on the ceiling. One looked like a cross between a human and a horse, with horns, a forked tail, hooves and breasts, *nursing a frickin' baby!* How had I not noticed that before?

I felt like garbage because my life was going further to shit. I'd gotten a text message from my literary agent, who informed me that *Hooked* had been rejected by every publishing house in Toronto — even by some that had not received the manuscript. How is that even possible? I needed the advance for *Hooked* to get me through the rest of the year. My agent said, "I didn't hook 'em" with my tales of terror involving a fly-in fishing hooker." Then he stopped returning my emails and phone calls. I was ghosted by my agent.

I needed a drink and felt compelled to go back downstairs to Romans. The doors were propped open to let in a breeze. Most of the tables were full. I grabbed the last free stool at the bar. Lucy looked my way and grinned. She was wearing impossibly tight black leather pants, those black stiletto boots and a leather vest with nothing underneath. Her entire outfit must have been sewed onto her body. I wasn't sure how she could move, or go to the bathroom. I wasn't sure she even went to the bathroom; it seemed beneath her.

She enticed and frightened me at the same time. I wasn't quite sure what I was doing there. I was separated, unemployed, living above a dive bar in a neighbourhood that time had forgotten and I was chasing a crush on a clairvoyant Gothic Cleopatra who frightened me.

Lucy poured me a Canadian Club on the rocks. I didn't even have to order. "How is your writing going?"

"I think I've got writer's block." I was lying, but I got a sense that she saw right through me, figuratively and, if I was being honest, literally.

"Is that what you call it?"

"Yeah, writer's block. You know, when you don't have any good ideas, when you can't figure out what to write."

Lucy looked at me the way a mother does when she knows her child is not being truthful. Damn it, what did she know?

"Well, if it's only writer's block, I may be able to help."

"Excuse me?"

"I have something to help with your . . . blockage," she said. "But you have to be committed. This is not for the weak of heart. All success comes with a price, doesn't it? Are you prepared to pay that price?"

"Yeah, I think so." I was desperate and she knew it. "With great talent comes great responsibility. Or something like that, right?"

"That's not what I'm talking about. Maybe this is too much for you."

"No, no, no!" I blurted. I needed to rescue this moment. "I'm a big boy. I can handle it."

Lucy stared at me intensely. Then her face slowly relaxed and she smiled. "I have a natural remedy that can release your creativity. It's an old-world formula that has been in my family for centuries. I come from a family of writers, too. Meet me here tomorrow night at closing."

Oh boy, what had I done? Maybe I couldn't handle this. I didn't know what to say, so I said nothing. But I couldn't seem to stop nodding my head.

* * *

I sat in my apartment the next morning with Lucy on my mind. I was still puzzled by her offer. Natural remedies? What was that? What did she mean by not being able to handle it? I felt like I needed a distraction. I wanted to do something fun — go on a date, meet somebody more like me. I hadn't been on a date since the last millennium. Everyone was talking about dating apps. After some superficial research, I downloaded one and created a profile. It was modest. I talked about my love of the outdoors, sports, books, my Royal Doulton collection — whatever might make me sound interesting. Then it was time to start swiping.

Jenny, brunette: *I like red wine, dinner with friends, travelling, hiking some far-off mountain, or feeling endless white sand between my toes. I am just as comfortable in a little black dress as I am in jeans and hiking boots.*

Marie, blonde, power suit: *When I'm not running my own architectural firm, I like to relax with close friends at the cottage, sip red wine, or visit the museums of Europe. I am just as comfortable in a little black dress as I am in jeans and barefoot on the dock, reading a good book.*

Kate, redhead: *I'm a teacher, and after a stressful day in the classroom, I like to curl up on the couch with my cat and a glass of red wine. I like travelling with my friends, running half marathons, and I'm just as comfortable in a black dress as I am in my Birkenstocks.*

Then I saw Mia's profile. She had short blonde hair and a healthy, wholesome smile, like she could be on a billboard advertising milk. I wondered what she'd look like with a milk mustache. *I'm divorced and am not really sure how to do this. But here we go. I'm a nurse who has worked mostly in developing countries the past few years. I've returned to Canada recently after deciding to stop running from my past. I've taken up tennis again. I believe in leaving the world a better place than I found it.*

Hmm. That was refreshing. I wanted to meet Mia. I swiped to the right. Then I tried to forget about it. I didn't want to get my hopes up. I hadn't had the best of luck with the ladies.

That night, I went downstairs to Romans around eleven. The place was mostly empty. Lucy was behind the bar. Her eyes sparkled as I took a seat.

"No alcohol tonight," she said. "I have something better for you later. We'll go up to your place."

My place? I wasn't sure that was such a good idea. It didn't matter, however, as I'd lost control of my responses again.

"Okay, sounds great," I said. "How about an iced tea, then?"

Lucy eventually closed the bar and looked at me with those hypnotic eyes, then she glanced toward the door. We walked up the dim stairwell to my apartment. I tried not to look embarrassed by its appearance. I'd tidied up and bought some vanilla-scented candles. I was really hoping the place didn't smell like a guy who'd been living for the past few weeks on Ruffles (sour cream 'n' onion, of course) and self-pity.

Lucy looked around. She seemed unfazed by the way I lived. "This is all you need, Mr. Colby." She walked over to the couch and sat down, setting a black leather bag on the floor. From the bag she pulled out a small brown jug.

"Please bring two shot glasses."

I didn't actually have two shot glasses, so I went for what seemed clean: a coffee mug and a glass measuring cup.

"It's warm in here," she said as she took off her jacket and poured a clear liquid into the glasses. "This is an elixir, a secret formula from the old country."

"Oh, really. Where is the old country?"

"Germany."

"Fehr. Of course, that makes sense. You said you come from a family of writers. Anyone I may have heard of?"

"Unlikely. Their writings were never translated or made available to the public. Their work was mainly read at secret gatherings. My family has always operated in the shadows. One had some fame, however. Google Gustav von Aschenbach sometime. The weak bastard."

"Gustav von who?"

"Never mind. Let's focus on why we are here. This potion will open you up to ideas and possibilities you never imagined. I will join you. You shouldn't do it alone."

She put her black lips to the I ♥ East Gwillimbury coffee mug, took a seductive sip and looked at me. "Your turn, Mr. Colby."

I had no idea what I was doing, but I was unable to say no. I knocked back the measuring cup. The drink had a slight bitterness. She refilled my cup.

"We have to do at least one more and then we'll go from there," she said.

I knew I should have stopped, but I couldn't. I tossed back the second drink. I felt nothing at first. Lucy got up and walked over to my bookshelf. Books were about all I had in the apartment.

"*Rosemary's Baby*. My favourite. *The Metamorphosis*. Ooh, creepy! Hmm. *Memoirs of a Geisha*. That's unfortunate." Then she grabbed *Death in Venice*. "Well, well, this is getting personal," she said cryptically. "Enough chit-chat," she snapped. "Round three." She marched to the couch and sat down beside me, her thigh pressed against mine.

She poured two more shots of her elixir, then reached over and gripped my hand. Her elegant fingers were stronger than I expected. My heart beat faster. I was feeling the effects of the drink now. My stomach and tongue started to tingle. The room began to shimmer and I felt a floating sensation.

Oh boy, I need to go home. Damn — I *am* home.

* * *

I gradually became aware of sunlight streaming into my bedroom through a crack in the curtains. My eyes slowly opened and I immediately realized something was wrong. Very wrong. I was covered in feathers. And I had wings. And yellow feet with three toes. This couldn't be.

"Lucy!" I warbled. No answer.

I strutted to the bathroom, my head bobbing back and forth and I looked in the mirror. Staring back at me were beady red eyes and a beak. My body was covered in slate blue feathers. My chest was ruby red. I had seen this bird before at the Royal Ontario Museum. I had become a passenger pigeon. Once the most abundant bird in the world, it became extinct more than a hundred years ago.

I walked back into the living room. There was no sign of Lucy and I had no memory after sitting on the couch. I spread out my wings and examined them. Impressive. What would happen if I flapped them, ever so slightly? I felt my feet get lighter as I rose a few millimetres off the floor. What if I flapped harder? The next thing I saw was the water-stained ceiling speeding toward my face.

Wham!

* * *

I was awakened from a deep sleep by three quick, deliberate raps at the door. Three weeks had passed and I still hadn't left my apartment. I'd ordered in groceries. Lots of seeds and nuts. I had them left outside the door. *The Etobicoke Guardian* had proven useful for lining the bathroom floor. I'd had visions, or dreams, every night of being a bird, so I'd started to write them down in a notebook I'd labelled *Hatched*. But I couldn't read it very well because it looked like chicken scratch. I was beginning to understand where that phrase came from.

There were three more deliberate raps on the door. Who could it be? I hadn't ordered more seeds.

"Just a minute," I chirped as I hopped to the door, which suddenly opened on its own.

I was met by the piercing gaze of coal-black eyes framed by pure white skin, long black eyelashes and pierced lips, nose and ears. A river of raven hair flowed over her shoulders.

"Lucy, my God," I clucked. "What are you doing here?"

"I came to check on you. You haven't been to Romans."

"Haven't been to Romans? Are you kidding me, Lucy? I'm a bird! What the hell did you do to me?"

"Oh, don't get your feathers all ruffled. I told you I'd give you something to write about. It worked famously for Kafka. Have you been writing?" She glanced at the table, saw the notebook and nodded approvingly. "See, it's working. I brought something for you to read."

"I don't really need any books right now. But I could really go for same acorns, now that I think about it."

Lucy's slim body slipped past me and she walked over to the couch and sat down. "Sit with me. I may have some sesame snaps in my bag."

I was feeling wobbly and finding a perch seemed like a good idea.

"I didn't bring you books," she said. "I brought you this to read instead." She reached in her bag and pulled out a white plastic stick with a blue handle. A blue plus sign was visible on the device's small screen.

I looked up at Lucy. "You're joking, right?"

"You're going to be a father."

"But we didn't even . . ."

"Oh, we did. Several times."

My head started to spin. I needed to sit down, but realized I was already sitting down.

"I thought you said that you like those twist endings, Mr. Colby — the ones you don't see coming."

* * *

I was awakened from a deep sleep by three quick, deliberate raps at the door. I had no idea what day or time it was. The apartment was unlit and it was dark outside except for the street lights. It appeared to be raining. I tried to get up but realized both my wrists were handcuffed to the bed. So were my legs. Fuzzy pink handcuffs. And I was naked.

From my bed, I could barely make out the door in the ambient light. The handle slowly turned and the door creaked open. My heart started to race. Why wasn't the door locked? In the doorway, silhouetted by the dim hallway light, was a slim female figure with long flowing hair and tall stiletto boots. She stepped inside and slowly closed the door behind her. She snapped the deadbolt shut and then carefully slipped the chain lock into its slot and slid it across.

I heard her boots clicking across the parquet floor. She stopped briefly at the bookshelf. I heard pages rustling. She walked into my room. The streetlight softly illuminated her ivory skin. Her black hair and leather clothing disappeared into the darkness of my room. I could see her white hands and elongated black fingernails holding a book. She pulled the small chair in my room to the side of the bed and sat down.

"I said I'd be back to check on you. Sorry about the handcuffs, but you were a flight risk. I think I like you better as a bird. It's okay, you don't have to talk."

I tried to talk but couldn't. What was happening?

Lucy was glowing. Her milky skin radiated in the darkness; her black eyes glistened.

"I thought I would read to you."

A feeling of dread overwhelmed me. Lucy's presence was not comforting.

"Remember my favourite book? *Rosemary's Baby.* How appropriate."

I tried to scream but nothing came out — except a single ruby-red feather, which slowly floated away into the darkness.

At that moment, the screen on my cellphone on the bedside table lit up. Lucy's fingers reached over and picked it up. I had a notification.

Congratulations! You have a new match! I saw Mia's smiling face.

A soft, ironic laugh escaped Lucy's mouth. "Yes, you do," she whispered. Lucy placed her hand on the phone's screen and swiped left. "Oh, look, another surprise!"

Mia's image disappeared from the phone. Lucy began to read and the last thing I saw was the fading glow of the phone before it was swallowed by the darkness.

* * *

I awoke and it was suddenly daytime and I was human, clothed in a purple velour track suit. It was rather slimming, in fact. Was this real? Was I hallucinating? The apartment door slowly opened, revealing a blinding white light. A man with round glasses, salt-and-pepper hair, a red velvet smoking jacket and paisley ascot appeared from out of nowhere. He was smiling — and shimmering. He was somewhat translucent, as if he were an apparition.

"Guten tag, Herr Colby," he said. "My name is Gustav von Aschenbach."

"Gustav von who?"

He tossed his head back and laughed. "I was told you'd be Googling my writing. Come with me. We can Google together. Forever."

II

Thunder Bay Trilogy

4

Royal Flush

(Originally published in The Feathertale Review, Vol. 9)

EXCLUSIVE

Monarchist arrested attempting to steal the Queen's DNA

Attired in the Union Jack, Nigel Preston shares twisted tale with Scott Colby moments before troubling incident

THUNDER BAY, ONTARIO, CANADA—It had been nearly thirty years since Queen Elizabeth II and Prince Philip last visited this isolated port city in the heart of the Canadian Shield and Nigel Preston realized this might be his last chance at redemption.

Preston is currently incarcerated and facing potential extradition to England, where a group of monarchists are advocating he be hanged, drawn and quartered for "gross disrespect to the Crown."

Preston was among the thousands yesterday who lined up for hours to get a front-row view of Her Majesty and her husband, the Duke of Edinburgh, during the recent opening of Queen Elizabeth Landing — a new waterfront park dedicated to the long-reigning monarch.

I met Preston moments before his arrest. He was pressed against the fencing where the Port Arthur Train Station once stood — a historic site where the Queen's parents, King George VI and Queen Elizabeth, visited in 1939 as part of a triumphant cross-Canada train tour.

It was Preston's appearance that first caught my attention. He looked like someone who had just walked out of a Monty Python skit. He was tall and lean, waving his Union Jack flag, wearing his Union Jack top hat, Union Jack bow tie, white gloves, and tuxedo with tails.

He said he was sixty-six years old and that he'd lived in the Lakehead region since the early 1970s. He reluctantly agreed to an interview as we waited for The Royals to open the new park and unveil a plaque.

SC: Nigel, you are clearly a big fan of the monarchy.

NP: I was born a British subject and I shall die a British subject.

SC: I see. So this must be a big day for you, then?

NP: Indeed, sir. I have fancied the Queen since I was a young boy growing up in Portsmouth during her father's reign.

SC: Did you come out to see the Queen during her visit here in 1973?

NP: I was unable to attend the ceremony. I was in the hospital, thanks to my wife. Atrocious woman, really.

SC: Your wife?

NP: Ex-wife. She overwhelmed me with a frying pan on the day of Her Majesty's last royal visit.

SC: She what?

NP: She hit me, sir, with a frying pan to the back of the head on my way out the door to greet the Queen. Do try to follow.

SC: Jesus, Nigel ...

NP: Knocked me out cold. It took twenty-two stitches to close the back of my head.

SC: Why on earth would your wife hit you with a frying pan?

NP: She was afraid, sir. Afraid, you see, that I'd do something like this. (*He grasps his lapels with his white-gloved hands and pumps out his chest with pride.*) She was scared

I'd embarrass myself or get arrested trying to meet the Queen and the Prince.

SC: Arrested?

NP: Indeed, good sir. I've been meaning to talk to Her Majesty for quite some time now.

SC: I don't follow.

NP: Right. You see, I have a bit of . . . hmm . . . How shall I put this? I have a history with the Queen.

SC: So you've met the Queen?

NP: Not directly, sir.

SC: So, indirectly?

NP: I worked on the *Britannia* for four years in the 1960s, before I moved to the Queen's Northern Dominion.

SC: You mean Canada?

NP: Thank you, but I prefer it my way.

SC: Right, okay. You said you worked on the Queen's boat?

NP: Ship! Her Majesty's Yacht *Britannia* was a ship. Not some common dinghy, sir. Please show her the respect she deserves.

SC: Oh. Sorry. I guess that means you travelled with the Queen?

NP: I only saw her from afar, when she boarded and disembarked, really. I was just a young servant boy. A cleaner in Her Majesty's employ. Told to mind my business and keep things tidy.

SC: So, you've never actually met the Queen, then?

NP: No, sir, but I carry a piece of her with me at all times.

SC: Come again?

NP: I have a piece of the Queen, sir.

SC: You what?

NP: Yes, sir, in my wallet at all times.

SC: You have a piece of the Queen? What, a baby tooth? A lock of her hair?

NP: You're closer with the second guess.

SC: You have the Queen's hair?

NP: Actually, it's only one hair, really. A token, which I plucked from the seat of her loo.

SC: Pardon me? Nigel, did you just say you have one of the Queen's, um, pubic hairs?

NP: Indeed. In my wallet.

SC: Umm ... hmm ... I guess it survived the royal flush, then? This might sound weird, but can I see it?

NP: (*Sighs.*) In for a penny, in for a pound. This is what I was afraid of. (*He reaches for his wallet.*) Here it is, my good man. I had it laminated.

SC: Mr. Preston, I . . . I almost hate to ask. But how is it that you have a laminated pubic hair in your wallet, which you claim belongs to the Queen of England?

NP: Lest you forget, sir, she is also the Queen of Canada.

SC: Right, sorry, the Queen of Canada. But please, how?

NP: Since you ask, I'll tell you. I was a loo cleaner on board the *Britannia*. One day, whilst steaming into port in India, I was waiting to clean the private suite shared only by the Queen and Prince Philip, but I was told the Queen was not yet done with the loo. And so I stood outside her chambers and waited, rather patiently. When finally her staff said Her Royal Highness had left, I entered her water closet — and there it was, sitting on the loo seat.

SC: So you took it?

NP: (*Nods with satisfaction.*)

SC: That's kind of disturbing.

NP: Young man: do be honest with yourself. Would you not have done the same in my stead?

SC: Umm …

NP: Bloody hell, it's the Queen's pubic hair! (*Looks around the crowd.*) Who else among us can say they have the Queen's pubic hair in their keeping?

SC: Keep your voice down! If they hear you they'll drag you out of here in handcuffs.

NP: Yes, that's exactly what my wife said in '73.

SC: Right, the frying pan.

NP: (*Comes closer to the microphone, lowering his tone to a whisper.*) Let me tell you, sir: the holding of this little laminated treasure has caused me many a problem these past forty-six years, but that's all going to change after today. You wouldn't believe it if I told you, sir, but I was actually dismissed from my post on the *Britannia* when I showed it to the other staff. They called me a liar, a pervert. A man unfit to serve Her Majesty. Me, unfit to serve Her Majesty? I think not. No one believed me. They still don't. But I tell you, this hair is the centrepiece of my royals collection. Sure, other monarchists have commemorative plates, spoons, programs, stamps, place-mats, posters, books. But this (*holds out the hair*), this distinguishes me. And yet, its very presence in my pocket has caused me to be ostracized by my peers, exiled to the nether regions of Her Majesty's realm, where even the local Monarchist League thinks me a nutter. They say I'm tawdry, vulgar and undignified. A pervert, even. But I know what I am. And so here I stand, in tails and top hat. This is my chance, sir, to prove once and for all that the hair in my wallet belonged to Her Majesty.

SC: Wait, Nigel — you're not planning to approach The Royals with your little treasure, are you?

NP: Oh, but I most certainly am. I need to know who used the bathroom last all those years ago. Was it the Queen or was it Philip?

SC: I have to say, Nigel, you have a look in your eye that's kind of disturbing. What is it you're planning to do?

NP: Extract their DNA.

SC: What?

NP: Do you not watch *CSI*, sir? I mean to snatch a hair off the Queen's coat. Short of that, I'll snatch one from her husband's. Only with a DNA sample from one of them will I be able to prove the legitimacy of my claim and redeem myself in the eyes of my fellow monarchists.

SC: Nigel, I'm not sure that's a good ...

LOUDSPEAKER: Ladies and gentlemen, we are proud to announce the arrival of Her Royal Highness, Queen Elizabeth II, Queen of Canada.

CROWD: (*Cheering.*)

SC: Nigel, I really don't think you should ...

NP: Here she comes.

SC: Nigel, don't!

RCMP: Move back, sir. Move back *now*.
NP: Get your hands off me!
SC: Oh, shit.

5

The Legend of Stump Foot

(Originally published in The Feathertale Review, Vol. 8)

As a seven-year-old, Savanne Lake was a magical place. Nestled in the heart of the Canadian Shield, it was a world of lakes and dense forest that seemed to extend to the ends of the Earth. My father's research station was a twenty-kilometre drive on a rugged, unmarked logging road off a lonely stretch of the Trans Canada Highway, 120 kilometres west of Thunder Bay.

Other than the six-bedroom trailer, there was no sign of civilization on Savanne Lake, or the next lake and many of the lakes after that. It was a world of wonderment. I marvelled at the fish my father studied, at the dancing blue-green curtain of the Northern Lights, at the moose, deer, eagles, lynx and at the metamorphosis of the tadpoles, which sprouted legs only to become kamikaze frogs, voluntarily leaping into the beach bonfire. It was a huge and boundless world.

That all changed one evening. I could not have known this world would collapse as dusk arrived and Savanne

Lake would undergo its own transformation to a place of blackness, of fear, of the unknown, where my sense of safety extended only to the edge of whatever light source we had, be it a bonfire or flashlight. It wasn't the foxes, bears, howling wolves or creepy-crawlies that struck fear. It was far worse: I had been initiated into the world of Stump Foot.

I was the youngest of three boys. We each had individual introductions to the deranged Finnish trapper who had lost his left leg in one of his bear traps. He fashioned a spruce tree into a leg and used a rusty chain to strap it onto his stump. But that wasn't good enough. Stump Foot wanted a fresh human leg and he stalked the woods of Northwestern Ontario at night searching for one.

My father had a PhD in fish biology and landed a job as a walleye expert for the Ontario government. In 1971 we packed our Ford station wagon and drove from the leafy college town of Ann Arbor, Michigan, two days north to Thunder Bay, a frontier city of paper mills, pulp trucks and grain elevators on the shores of Lake Superior. I wasn't happy about the move, leaving my friends behind for this pickup truck and lunch-bucket crowd in the remote Canadian wilderness.

One aspect of Thunder Bay life I did embrace, however, was fishing. That first summer in Thunder Bay, my father would take the entire family out to Savanne on weekends, when the other biologists and students came back to town. We'd fish for walleye and big northern pike and swim in the dark lake. There was no running water, no TV, no stereo, no phone and no heat. The only contact to the outside world were transistor radios and a CB radio, for emergencies such as forest fires. Our luxuries were a gas stove and fridge, stinky outhouse and a terribly loud generator on the hill several hundred metres away that had to be shut off each night, plunging the compound into darkness. At that point the only illumination came from the moon, flashlights or bonfires. Even though it became spooky at night, the sky was always a thrill, filled with stars and galaxies: the glowing Milky Way stretched across the sky, satellites raced overhead, shooting stars and the aurora borealis inspired awe.

We sometimes went to Savanne during the week and got to know my father's staff. My favourites where Hugh and Vie: a one-two combination of laughs and hijinks. It was the early seventies and Vie sported long hippie hair, while Hugh grew a thick, dark beard. Vie was hoping to get into dental school and I became his first patient when he helped remove a wobbly tooth.

It was the next summer when Stump Foot entered our world. One night after dinner, Vie took me to the back porch and my initiation had suddenly arrived.

* * *

A short dirt trail leads to the outhouse and beyond that is a hill thick with trees. The sun has just disappeared behind the trees and twilight is upon us. Vie guides me to face the hill and points to the tall poplars.

"Scott, you see that?" he asks, pointing upwards.

It is calm where we stand, but fifty feet up, the wind batters the poplar leaves, sounding like a distant waterfall.

"The sky is clear and there will be full moon. You know what that means, Scott?"

I look at Vie, not understanding.

"These are kind of the nights when Stump Foot likes to travel."

A cold shiver runs down my back.

"I know you've heard of Stump Foot from your brothers. He's nocturnal, Scott. That means he's active at night. He's disgusted by his deformity and doesn't want to be seen, so he needs moonlight to travel and check his traps. But it was exactly one of those traps that ruined him," Vie explained.

"He wasn't paying attention and his left leg stepped in the middle of one of his bear traps. It was late fall, just before the hibernation and an early blizzard surprised him. His leg was in the trap and if he spent the night, he'd freeze to death. So he cut his own leg off with a saw."

Vie tells how the trapper fashioned a wooden leg out of a spruce tree and attached it to his stump with a chain. All this time in the woods alone, combined with his deformity, has driven him crazy. The wooden leg isn't good enough — he wants a human leg.

"If Stump Foot visits, there is a way to fool him, however. You must put a pillow over your left leg so if he pulls back your sleeping bag and sees the pillow, he'll think you don't have a left leg and will leave you alone."

"That really works?" I ask. That doesn't seem right.

"Yes, it does. He's crazy, remember and doesn't reason very well. The good thing is Stump Foot is easily fooled."

"Oh yeah, one more thing," Vie says as he crouches beside me. "You can hear him coming. He has a distinctive walk. He steps with his good leg and then drags his bad leg and rusty chain behind him. It's kind of a thump, drag, rattle! It will give you time to check your pillow."

This is not very comforting. You can hear this terrible man coming with his thumping and rattling and he will enter your room and pull back your sleeping bag!

Darkness falls on Savanne Lake as the full moon creeps above the trees, spreading a golden beam across the still lake. My father says he's going to turn off the generator. "Want to come with me?"

"What about Stump Foot?"

"You don't believe that, do you?"

"But Hugh and Vie say it's true."

"I don't think we'll see Stump Foot turning off the generator," my father says, handing me a second flashlight. "Let's go."

We march up the dirt road. The road climbs a steep hill. We dodge the gullies carved by summer storms, careful to watch our step in the searching beams of the flashlights. The road curves to the left and at the top of the hill, nestled in the opening of the forest, is the roaring generator, the building's lights illuminating the woods. My father opens the door. The sound is deafening. He turns the key and the engine shakes and jolts as it comes to a stop. The forest is immediately cloaked in darkness and silence.

This is the part I hate: the walk back. In such darkness, the flashlights cast spooky shadows and strange sounds can be heard deep in the woods. The camp is dark. I go

to my room at the back of the camp, two doors down from my father's, and close the door. The doors don't have locks. I set the flashlight on the bedside table and pull down the window blind. I change into my PJs and crawl into the cool sleeping bag, grab my pillow and shove it down the bag to cover my left leg. I lean back, roll over and turn off the flashlight. The room is black. I lie on my back and realize how uncomfortable it is to sleep without a pillow.

I don't know how long I lay there but sleep does not come easily as I listen for sounds. At one point I wake up, notice my pillow has slipped off my left leg, adjust it and fall asleep.

My eyes open again and I realize it's morning. The muted daylight peeks through the slats in the blinds and catches the steely edge of the large knife on the bedside table.

I bolt upright. Stump Foot has been here!

I recognize the knife. It's the largest one from the camp kitchen. I thought Stump Foot brought his own. I hear the sounds and smells of bacon frying, grab the knife and stride to the kitchen.

"Stump Foot was here last night!" I shout to Hugh and Vie and the other crew, holding up the knife.

"The pillow trick worked, didn't it?" Hugh says.

"Well, yeah, I guess so. Did you hear anything? Did he visit your rooms?"

"No, we didn't hear a thing," Vie says. "We all must have slept pretty hard. It's a good thing he falls for the pillow trick."

The crew doesn't seem worried. My father comes in from shaving. He's not concerned either. How can they not be terrified of a bloodthirsty Finnish trapper walking around the camp at night?

It is a typical day at Savanne Lake: fishing, skipping stones, reading comics, studying the weather equipment in the office. We follow the same routine at night. Time to turn off the generator. I grab my flashlight and anxiously follow my father. Back at the camp, I return to my room, climb in my sleeping bag, put the pillow on my left leg and turn out the flashlight. I somehow fall asleep.

My eyes open. What was that? Did I hear something?

It's coming from the roof. I hear the thump of a heavy boot on the aluminum roof! Something is being dragged and then the rattle of a chain. Thump! Drag! Rattle!

Stump Foot! He's on the roof!

Thump. Drag. Rattle. He's above my room!

I click on the flashlight, sprint out the door and race down the hall to my father's room.

"Dad! It's Stump Foot!" I dive into his bed.

"I know. Scary isn't it? We'll be safe, Scott. I've got my hunting rifles."

Stump Foot rattles around the roof for a bit and to my great relief, eventually leaves.

The next day my mind tries to process Stump Foot. A lot of this isn't making sense. The outside doors to the camp lock, but somehow he can get in, but sometimes he can't. Why is he so easily fooled by the pillow? How exactly does a chain hold on his wooden leg? My father surely wouldn't put his children in such danger. This must be some kind of prank.

Hugh and Vie answer my questions and sense my doubt. Evening arrives and Vie tells me it's time for a boat ride.

My father and I take one boat while Hugh and Vie pilot *The Loon Shit*, a large boat used to haul nets.

We motor north about twenty minutes to the end of the lake, an area I know well. Hugh guides *The Loon Shit* onto a narrow rocky beach while Vie ties the rope to a log. My dad pulls up beside them and I jump off the bow with the rope and tie a slip knot around another tree.

"Follow us," Vie says as he disappears down a narrow trail. I've never seen this trail before. We walk on the soft mossy ground for a few minutes, pushing branches out of the way. Around a turn is a small two-room cabin.

Hugh and Vie walk in.

"Who lived here?" I ask my father. "It looks abandoned."

"Let's go in and find out."

I tentatively step through the doorway and see a small room with an old iron stove, handmade table and a wall calendar from a Thunder Bay insurance company. The year: 1951. The shelves are barren except for a mug, some matches, a salt shaker and container of Magic Baking Soda.

Really? Magic? I inspect the label. It looks new and something Hugh or Vie could not have made. Holy shit.

My father calls me into the bedroom. "Have a look in here, Scott."

The bedroom is small with a wooden bunk, an empty shelf and hanging on the wall, on a large iron nail, is a long red and grey woolen sock.

"This is Stump Foot's cabin," Vie exclaims. "See, one sock."

Double holy shit. I'm convinced. There is a Stump Foot! "Where is he?" I urgently ask.

"He has several of these cabins across the region," Hugh explains. "One for each of his trap-lines. He must have taken his things and left last night. Who knows when he'll be back."

The sun is already behind the trees and it is getting dark as we walk back to the boats. There is tightness in my chest and a chill on my skin.

Stump Foot's visits were sporadic that summer and the next, but when we least expected it: Thump! Drag! Rattle! One memorable night, he rattled through the camp for the first time and past my door, but didn't come in. On another occasion all three sons ended up in my father's bed as Stump Foot banged around the kitchen and then dragged and rattled down the hall. We tried to come up with plans to stop him. Couldn't we put Ping-Pong balls all over the hallway floor so he'd slip and fall? What about trip lines attached to empty cans to warn us when he approached the camp?

But my brother Craig had a different idea. "Maybe he just needs a friend. What if we put out cookies for him and a note?"

"Are you crazy?" I said. "You can't be friends with him. He'll kill you and cut off your leg."

At the end of the second summer of Stump Foot, he decided to visit early one night. The entire family was out this time and we were all still up when we were alerted to the distinctive thump, drag, rattle coming from the bush.

* * *

It is raining lightly and all five of us gather on the front porch. You can barely see Stump Foot. He is lurking in the shadows, at the edge of the light cast from the porch light.

Someone has a flashlight and shines it at him. Stump Foot turns his back, which is covered in a bear skin. He pulls it up to cover his head. It is our first sighting.

Craig suddenly bolts down the steps and into the rain and darkness. "I think he just needs a friend."

What the . . .? "Craig!" we yell.

Too late to stop him, Craig heads right at Stump Foot, who turns his back again and starts to run.

Craig catches up.

I'm stunned, mesmerized by such a bold and dangerous stunt. Craig reaches up and pulls off the bearskin.

"Hey, it's Hugh," Craig shouts.

A familiar face turns toward the light, revealing Hugh's bright, bearded smile.

"I knew it was fake," I holler, jumping up and down. "I knew it must be one of you guys."

"Is that why you always jumped in your dad's bed," a laughing Vie says as he comes around the side of the camp, swinging a stubby of Carling O'Keefe beer. I have no defence.

In one unexpected moment, Stump Foot is exposed and the reign of terror is over. But so is some of the mystique of Savanne Lake.

The last time I was at Savanne was 1991, bird hunting with my father. By this point we had hot water showers and the generator ran all night, so electricity 24/7. We may have talked of Stump Foot that outing, I'm not sure, but my father had insisted for years that he, Hugh and Vie were just as surprised as me to see that single red-and-grey sock hanging on the old iron nail.

Five years later funding was cut to my father's research station and everything was hauled out of the bush. Today there is only a dirt road and a clearing where the research station once stood and a narrow beach where walleye still spawn when the ice melts. But I'm sure Stump Foot's cabin is still there in the thick woods, maybe with one sock hanging on a nail and if you listened hard enough the faint echo of his haunting thump, rattle, drag echoing through the poplars on a clear summer evening, when the moon is full.

6

Under the I: Memoirs of a Teenage Bingo Caller

(Originally published in The Feathertale Review, Vol. 6)

I dread walking up the stairs to the Port Arthur Community Centre bingo. Waiting for me is a hellish, hazy hall of smoldering cigarettes smoked by a miserable ensemble of blue-haired ladies, grumpy old men and candy-chewing cows. It is easy to imagine how the condemned man must feel as he is forced to climb the stairs of the gallows. But for him, at least, there will be quick relief to his torment.

Saturday Night Bingo is the last place I want to be. But at seventeen, it is not like my weekends are filled with great adventures, or many minor adventures, for that matter. Quitting this job in some legendary fashion is my favourite teenage fantasy — at least it is at 5:55 on a Saturday evening.

The lure of making a little cash, however, is too great. I come back to this carcinogenic cavern that burns the eyes and throat from the outside while it corrodes the soul from within. These pathetic denizens, who cough and grumble and limp and burn us with their cigarettes as we collect money, who gamble away their meagre earnings in the hopes of winning the elusive $100 jackpot, are a sad excuse for retirement. They don't even realize they are already dead. If this isn't hell, it must be the foyer.

On this fateful fall evening, as I force my feet up each step, there is no way I could know that my reprieve is imminent; that it will be my last night in bingo purgatory.

Saturday Night Bingo is a fundraiser for the community centre. At least some good comes out of this misery. It also pays well, usually $16 for a four-hour shift. That's $4 an hour, significantly more than minimum wage — $2.85 for those of us under 18. On good nights, when the hall is packed, we might make $18. On rare occasions, such as the last bingo before Christmas, we earn a princely payout of $20. The slowest nights yield $12. That puts a serious crimp into my strict money-saving strategy of putting away at least $10 a week from bingo toward university. I've been working here since I was 15. Thankfully, bingo isn't my only income. I've been mowing lawns since I was 12 and last year I landed a well-paying gig at the A&P stocking shelves, cleaning floors and bagging groceries for $6.50 an hour.

I work at the A&P most Saturday evenings, but not tonight. It's my first bingo in a month. I'm greeted by Louie, a crusty old Frenchman who is the ringleader

of this circus that is mostly freak show but lacking in acrobats. A petite man, he presides over the madness with a sharp-tongue, nervous energy and his fashionable cigarette extenders.

Several hundred players squeeze into the five rows of tables that fill the long hall above the swimming pool. Our main job is to collect the money from players for each round and read back the winning card to Louie, who calls the numbers for the first three hours. The first hour of rapid-fire rounds is the worst. Winners only need to fill one row of their card, either vertically, horizontally or diagonally. It costs 5 cents a card for the one-row games. Some ladies play thirty cards. Collecting the change is no easy feat. Sometimes we are halfway down the aisle when a winner is called and we must rush collection as Louie and the other players give us the hairy eyeball.

Players are supposed to set out the money for each round. For those playing a few cards, no problem, but collecting from big-time players requires counting rows of cards and making quick calculations. Some have a pile of coins and say take what you need, which is time consuming.

We quickly learn how to stack the quarters first, then the nickels and then the dimes in our left hand as we collect with our right. It is miserable, fast-paced work. The aisles are crowded and we have to reach over people to get their money. A burning cigarette to the forearm is a frequent job hazard; so common, an apology is rarely offered.

We bring the money back to the kitchen window and stack it to be counted by the two angels in this hell hole: Mrs. Heinonen and her sister Mrs. Maki. We love them and not just because they dole out our pay at the end of each night. They are always smiling and seem, well, normal.

The first hour is followed by two hours of two-line rounds. The price per card goes up, as do the payouts. The pace slows and we are now required to make change and play waiter, fetching pop, candy and coffee from the modest store at the back.

My buddy Bobby, our group's social director and a fledgling businessman, is responsible for us working there. He understands the value of making money as a teenager in Thunder Bay and is not afraid of hard work. Besides Bobby, my basketball teammate Darren also works there as does my oldest friend Andre. The camaraderie makes it almost bearable. When Bingo ends at 10 p.m. we immediately flee to The Strip — Red River Road — to spend some of our hard-earned cash.

It is a short walk and the first stop is always McDonald's. Next door is a Robin's Donuts, Gino's Pizza and Golden Dragon Chinese Restaurant, which has the latest video games, such as Space Invaders, Tron, Ms. Pac-Man and our favourite, a pirated version of Donkey Kong. The Strip is where the action is, where tough guys park their cars facing the street with the hoods up, where there is drinking in the darkened parking lots, where dope deals go down, where we see rival athletes and where we ogle the Deadly Bettys from other high schools, who always seem more exotic than the girls from our school. This is what we focus on as we toil in that sarcophagus among the living dead.

As a teenager, any trust placed in us by an authority figure is vital to our maturation on that rocky road to adulthood: a first job; passing the driver's test; getting the car for a date; being allowed to stay home alone. Louie bestowed such a gift on me when he asked me to be one of the students allowed to call the final two bingos of the evening.

I cannot overstate the significance of such a gesture from Louie, for him to share his power. Louie runs the bingo as a personal fiefdom. Calling bingo is his life's calling. And Louie is at the height of his powers when he sits at the front of the hall behind the whirring, popping bingo ball machine. This is King Louie's throne. It is his bridge, his cockpit, his chariot.

With authority he reads each number into the microphone. His voice booms throughout the hall, through the smoke and the grumbling and munching on Snicker's bars and Old Dutch potato chips. "Under the B — 5." "Under the O — 62." "Bingo!" "We have a bingo! Table 2!"

But what grudgingly makes Louie a legend are his trademark lines. Some numbers are special and deserve extra attention.

It is not, "Under the B — 1."

The hall comes alive with Louie's booming, "Wee Jimmy! B-1!

A favourite is, "Pension time, O-65."

There is also, "Heinz 57, G-57," for its 57 flavours.

"Clickety-click 66, O-66."

"Sweet 16, I-16."

"N-40, life begins at 40."

And "B8, skate and donate."

My favourite is "I-18, don't ya wish ya were."

YES I DO! But in this graveyard of broken dreams, his line is more of an indictment than a wish and it always produces a wave of grumbles. Louie, to his credit, smiles every time.

A few of us veterans are allowed to call the final two bingos — they are full houses and require every number on the card to win. Full houses, which take slightly less than 30 minutes to play, are important. They are the Stanley Cup of Saturday Night Bingo. Some players have been there for years and have never won the coveted full house. The victor earns $100, or more. But it does not end there: a win also includes "double good neighbours a dollar each." Unofficially, that means the two neighbours to the left and right get a dollar each. But that is not enough for Louie. He might pay two dollars. And it doesn't end there. The player directly across usually gets five dollars, and their neighbours receive a dollar each. That makes you one popular winner.

The two hours of two-line bingos are winding down and Louie motions me over to his throne. He asks me to call the final full houses. Great! An easy last hour. The key to calling them is finding the right rhythm; understanding how long it takes for hard-core players to scan up to thirty cards but not making six-card players wait too long. It's a tight-rope walk. After years of working there you get a feel for the crowd.

The first full house goes as planned. After about twenty-five minutes I hear the tell-tale rumbles. Someone is close to winning. "Under the G — 50." "Bingo!" "We have a winner, Table 4." Darren walks over and calls back the card. Each number is legit. Winners are happy. The others are silent or bemoan their luck. Better luck next time.

Time for the final full house. It's 9:30 and the place is still packed. I've returned the balls to the hopper and flick the switch. The painted ping-pong balls bounce to life and the first one quickly fires into the chute.

"Under the B — 4."

I look into the crowd, pacing my calls as another ball is sucked into the chute.

"Under the G — 55."

And so it goes. The crew is cleaning up, the money is being counted in the kitchen.

"Under the B — 7."

Andre grabs a chair and sits beside me. He's done for the night. "Under the O," there is a pregnant pause as I show the ball to Andre. We share a sly smile. Oh, how I'd love to boom out, "PENSION TIME. O-65!" But I don't dare. "Under the O — 65," I dead pan.

A few months ago, Joey from the Catholic high school did the unthinkable. On a final full house, he paused half-way through a call, looked at the ping-pong ball, glanced up at the crowd and then swallowing hard, offered his best, "Wee Jimmy, B-1!" It was more croak than declaration, but the hall erupted nonetheless. Some loved it, thinking Joey was honouring Louie. The cynics, however, smelled a fink. Joey was mocking Louie. Shame! We students were stopped in our tracks, slack jawed. "Whaa... He didn't."

Then a crimson wave rolled up Joey's neck, to his face and disappeared into his brown hair. Joey carried on, but he was visibly shaken, like a camper who survives an encounter with a bear at night on the way to the outhouse.

"Under the O — 70," I continue. "Under the B — 11."

The numbers fire out. The crowd is focused. "Under the G — 58."

The big clock behind me clicks off another minute. I look back, it reads 9:56. The tension is building. You can touch it in the toxic air.

"Under the N — 44."

Mumbles of an imminent bingo ricochet across the hall. Andre and I raise our heads, scanning the rows of tables for a bingo! I pause for a few extra seconds, then grab the next ball.

"Under the I — 23."

Louder murmurs tumble across the hall. Andre scans the tables. I follow his gaze. Nothing. But it is close. Very close.

"Under the B — 5."

"BINGO!"   "BINGOO!"   "BIIING-GOO!"   "BINGO!" "bingo."   "Bingo!"   "BINGO!" "BBBBBBBBBIIIIIIIIINNNNNNNNGGGGGGOOO!"

The hall explodes. There appear to be eleven freaking bingos. You might rarely see two full-house winners. But ELEVEN. It's unheard of. The students spring to action and fan out across the hall to read back the cards, yelling above the hoots and hollers. Oh, this isn't good. This will either break poor Louie's bank, or the payouts will be only $10 each and no one will be happy. I try to focus and diligently confirm each number. Yep, one winner. Yep, two winners. Yep, three winners.

Then Louie rushes to the front, waving his arms. "Stop! Stop! There was a winner TWO NUMBERS ago!" He rapidly reads back the card as the howls grow louder. "Yep, Louie, she's a winner."

I look at Andre. He shakes his head in disbelief. I turn off the microphone and return the balls to the hopper. "Bullshit," I mutter to myself. Andre and I are confident nobody called Bingo! two numbers ago. It probably took the old bat two extra numbers to read her cards.

Louie is clearly both agitated and relieved. One winner, thankfully, not eleven. But the hall is still filled with angry old people.

Thirtysomething Elinor, the only worker who is not a student, rushes over. "Andre was distracting you. He should never have been sitting there."

"Yeah," says her mother, a long-time player at Table 4. "Andre was distracting you."

"Oh come on, you can't be serious," Andre says.

Others join the chorus. "He shouldn't have been there. He was a distraction."

I look at the angry faces. "No, Andre was not a distraction. If anything, he was helping me."

"No he wasn't. He was a distraction," Elinor yells.

"You were a distraction," another bellows at Andre.

A feeling of calm suddenly comes over me. I rise from Louie's pulpit and step into the aisle. Andre is in front of me and we slowly walk the gauntlet. We are jeered and hissed at. A crumpled candy wrapper bounces off my arm. A crushed Styrofoam coffee cup sails past our heads. We keep our heads high and march to the back and greet Mrs. Heinonen and Ms. Maki.

"Hi there, ladies," Andre says. "How much did we make tonight?"

Mrs. Maki smiles and slides us each a $10 bill, a $2 bill and four $1 bills.

"Thank you, ma'am. Have a nice night."

"Yes, thank you," I say, then look back, "You two keep well, okay?"

I pull on my football jacket and bound down the stairs with Andre, Bobby, Darren and Joey, leaving the angry mob behind. "Enough of this crap."

We step into the crisp, clean November air. I pull my jacket tight against the wind that blows leaves across the parking lot and search the clear sky for the Northern Lights.

We head to The Strip.

Louie has it wrong. It should be, "I — 17. Thank God I am."

About the Author

Death in Etobicoke and Other Humorous Tales is Scott's second book. He is also the co-author, with NHL hockey dad Karl Subban, of the national best-selling memoir, *How We Did It: The Subban Plan for Success in Hockey, School and Life* (Penguin Random House Canada, 2017) and "That's What You Think: A Practical Guide to Writing Compelling Op-Eds and Short Memoirs" (2023). Scott has worked for newspapers for more than 35 years — as a reporter, photographer, designer, columnist and editor. He is currently the Opinions Editor at the Toronto Star. He lives in Toronto with his wife, daughter and son.

You can connect with me on:

- https://coachcolby.me

www.ingramcontent.com/pod-product-compliance
Lightning Source LLC
Chambersburg PA
CBHW021341060726
47591CB00006B/2133